the Cheetah Girls

the Cheetah ★ Girls

Original Movie Junior Novelization
Screenplay by Alison Taylor
Adapted by Jasmine Jones
Based on *The Cheetah Girls* by Deborah Gregory

Watch it on
Disney CHANNEL
abc Kids

Disney PRESS

VOLO

Printed in the United States of America

First Edition
1 3 5 7 9 10 8 6 4 2

Library of Congress Control Number: 2004112382

ISBN: 0-7868-4713-1

For more Disney Press fun, visit www.disneybooks.com
Visit DisneyChannel.com

the Cheetah Girls

●❀●❀●❀●❀●❀●❀●❀●❀●❀●❀●❀●

Chanel stepped to the front of the stage as she belted out the chorus of the Cheetah Girls' anthem, "Together." Behind her, Galleria, Dorinda, and Aquanette sang backup and worked their tight choreography.

Galleria grinned as the crowd started getting into it, clapping along to the bouncy beat. This is it, she thought as she started the next verse, the Manhattan premiere of our first hit.

So, okay, they were performing at a backyard party for a bunch of ten-year-old boys, one of whom was Chanel's little brother, Pucci. But *what-ever*. They were performing, weren't they? This was the Cheetah Girls' dream, and they were living it.

Chanel and Galleria leaned together, blending their voices in pitch-perfect harmony. They'd been best friends forever, since the days when they were both wearing designer diapers.

Galleria stepped forward again to let fly with her solo, just as Aqua let out a small cry—the heel of her white cowboy boot was wedged between two wooden slats on the deck. As Chanel tried to help Aqua free her shoe, Dorinda let loose a one-armed cartwheel and smacked right into them.

The boys went wild—laughing and jeering. Clueless, Galleria kept right on singing. At last, Aqua managed to yank her leg free, and the other two Cheetah Girls hauled her toward Galleria just in time to hit their final pose. The boys at the party cheered like mad.

They love us! Galleria thought, unaware that the boys were laughing and hooting for all the wrong reasons. The Cheetahs have been unleashed!

❖ ❖ ❖

"So we had some technical difficulties," Galleria protested moments later, when the other girls explained the disaster that had happened behind her back. They headed over to the snack table as the boys hurried toward the piñata.

"That's never happened before!" Chanel insisted as she scooped a handful of cheese puffs out of a bowl. "I call it a sign. Maybe we're not ready for the talent show audition tomorrow."

"Chanel, listen to me," Galleria said. "You finally hit that high C in the second chorus. Never happened before! I call that a sign that we *are* ready."

Chanel crinkled her nose. "I did?"

Aqua nodded.

"I did, huh?" Giggling, Chanel and Dorinda exchanged the Cheetah Girls hand-shake.

"We hung in there like pros," Galleria announced. "Aqua, even barefoot and hungry, girl, you kept the harmonies tight."

"Well, you know how we do it in Texas," Aqua said with a smile. Aqua had moved to New York City a few months earlier, and even though her parents had taken the girl out of Texas, they sure hadn't taken Texas out of the girl. "Always ride with your spurs on, girls."

Galleria turned to Dorinda. "And Do-Re-Mi is sore now, but you gave a hundred and ten percent to the fans. How does that feel?"

Dorinda smiled and flipped her long blond hair over her shoulder. "It was fun. And the bruises, they're not that bad."

"Right!" Galleria chirped. "Now if there is one person who doubts we can be the first freshmen to win the Manhattan Magnet School talent show, speak now or forever hold your peace."

Just then, the piñata got a serious whack attack, and a shower of candy rained down on Galleria's head.

Shrieking and giggling, the Cheetah Girls ducked away from the flying candy. Galleria grimaced as she peered down at the Tootsie

Roll that had plopped into the cup of juice in her hand. Plucking it out, she ripped off the wrapper and popped the candy into her mouth. "I take a whacking and keep on smacking," she said. "And I'm going to be a star. Now am I solo, or are you Cheetahs ready to blow up big-time?"

The Girls grinned at one another. "Cheetahs!" they cheered, clinking their cups of juice.

There was no doubt about it—the Cheetahs were ready to prowl.

"Lights out by nine-thirty," Galleria instructed later that day as the Cheetahs strutted down the street.

"I've got lessons at the youth center and tons of homework," Dorinda said. She nodded at a city bus that had just pulled to a stop at the curb. "If I miss this bus today, I'll be officially late for school tomorrow."

Galleria's perfectly arched eyebrows flew up. "Lessons? You need to rest those legs."

Dorinda huffed in frustration. All of the

Cheetahs knew that Dorinda's lessons were important to her—she was a serious dancer. That was why she had the smoothest moves in the group, and was their unofficial choreographer. What they *didn't* know was that Dorinda also had a job at the youth center— cleaning the floors after her dance class. That was how she paid for the lessons. And the other Cheetahs weren't going to find out, if she could help it.

"Let the girl take her lessons," Aqua said, knocking Galleria lightly on the shoulder.

Galleria sighed. "Okay. I'll e-mail you what we're going to wear."

"No!" Dorinda said quickly. "Because . . . uh, my computer is still down. Just give it to me tomorrow." She sprinted toward her bus, then flipped a cartwheel. "See!" she called over her shoulder, punching the air as she trotted away. "Right back in action. Bye!"

The Cheetahs cracked up.

"That girl is always on the move," Galleria said with a grin.

"Wait, taxi!" Aqua called, waving limply at

a yellow cab. A horn blared as the cab drove off in a streak of yellow. "It's called having a life, and I've got one, too," Aqua told Galleria. "My trig class at NYU starts in ten minutes."

"You've been in New York six months, and you're still scared to ride the subway?" Chanel asked.

Aqua rolled her eyes. "I told my daddy I'd live in New York," she replied. "I didn't say anything about *under* New York. It's dark and dirty and there's mole people down there." She shuddered at the thought of the horrors beneath her feet.

"Girl, whatever," Chanel said as she stepped off of the curb. "Learn this, Einstein-ette." Sticking two fingers in her mouth, she let out an ear-blasting whistle.

A cab screeched to a halt in front of her. "But you do have to get the door yourself, you know," Chanel joked.

Aqua gave her a look as she pulled an antibacterial hand-wipe out of her bag and used it to clean the door handle. "Remember me," Aqua said, handing the used wipe to Chanel.

"Thank you," Chanel said sarcastically as the cab pulled away. "Princess High of the Land of Maintenance!"

Galleria smiled as she and Chanel fell into step. "I know," Galleria admitted, "but she makes me giggle, and she's got the lungs of life!" Exchanging a look, she and Chanel burst into a high note, then dissolved into laughter.

"It's so hard with four girls," Chanel said, only half complaining. "It was easier when the Cheetah Girls was just you and me, girl. Divas in diapers."

Galleria gave a knowing nod. "But you know, Drinka was right when she said we needed backup." Drinka Champagne was the music teacher at Manhattan Magnet, their high school. "Now with Aqua and Do, we look and sound like a real girl group."

A worried frown crossed Chanel's face as she remembered the talent show auditions. "What about tomorrow? Girl, I don't want to get crunched like corn chips."

"We've got what it takes, Chuchie," Galleria said, using her pet name for her best friend. "The rest is all attitude. So when you get wobbly, just think about the dream. Girl, we could be grabbing Grammys!" Galleria waved as though she was up on stage, picking up her golden statue.

Following her lead, Chanel blew kisses to the imaginary crowd. "Thank you! Thank you so much!" she gasped. "We love you up there in the back row!"

Galleria took a bow, then turned to her friend. "Picture us juggling calls from the hot producers—Rodney Jerkins, Babyface, Jackal Johnson . . ."

"And the hot designers are calling us," Chanel agreed. She held her pinky and thumb to her ear, phone style, and added, "and we're all, 'Not now, Dolce, I'm talking to Gabbana on the other line!'"

"Hello?" Galleria pretended to pick up the phone. "One moment, please. Chuchie, it's Gucci . . . line one."

"Oh, no!" Chanel said in mock horror. "I

wear Prada or nada, mama!" She grabbed her best friend's hand. "Girl, you promise me when we're rich, we'll buy a penthouse apartment first thing? For you and me. Friends forever."

Galleria smiled, then wrapped Chanel in a warm hug. "Forever," she promised.

"Hold up!" Chanel said, catching sight of a life-sized photo in a record-store window. "There's Scherezade! Jackal Johnson's new girl!"

"I love her!" Galleria gasped.

"That's my video, girl. She's like . . ." Chanel let out a whoop and started to groove, clapping in time to the beat in her head. She and Galleria busted Scherezade's moves, shaking their shoulders and sliding across the pavement. In no time, a small crowd had gathered to watch them dance. The audience burst into applause as Galleria and Chanel finished their routine. "Thank you!" Galleria cried. "You'll see our picture in this window soon! Watch out for—"

At the edge of the crowd, a small white dog

let out a yip, and Galleria's eyes grew wide. "Oh my goodness! Toto!" she cried, suddenly remembering her own dog. "It's way past time to walk him! My mom is gonna blast me." Grabbing her friend by the wrist, Galleria started to haul Chanel away. "Come on, Chuchie!"

Galleria and Chanel broke into a run. The Cheetah Girls hated to rush—but this was a serious doggie emergency!

2

🐾 🐾 🐾 🐾 🐾 🐾 🐾 🐾 🐾 🐾 🐾 🐾 🐾 🐾 🐾

"The prodigal daughter has returned," Dorothea Garibaldi, Galleria's mother, said into the phone as she caught sight of Galleria slipping into the apartment. Hanging up, she folded her arms and raised her eyebrows at Galleria. Dorothea was tall and imposing, and always fabulously dressed. She had been a model before she had Galleria. Now she owned a boutique called Toto in New York . . . Fun in Diva Sizes.

"I'm so sorry I'm late!" Galleria said, giving her mother a guilty look.

"Oh, don't apologize to me," Dorothea said as she rolled up a gorgeous bolt of gold silk.

"I think you should talk to Toto. I can take myself to the bathroom, thank you."

Just then, a fluffy white bichon frise galloped into the living room, barking and wagging his tail at the sight of Galleria, who leaned down to pet him. "I'm so sorry, Pastamuffin! This is the last time—I promise I won't forget you again."

Dorothea gave her daughter a stern look. "This is the last time I do your chores."

"Mom, look, I know I've been really busy, but—" Galleria flashed her mother a confident grin. "The talent show audition is tomorrow. I promise you, it's going to pay off."

Dorothea nodded. "Pay," she repeated. "That's exactly what I wanted to talk to you about. Constellation Jones? When were you going to tell me she called to reschedule her fitting?"

Galleria gasped. "I didn't tell you about that one?" she asked. "I thought I wrote it down . . . Wait!" She scurried over to her book bag and dug around inside for her notebook. "Let me check the pad." Turning the page, she stabbed at the notebook with a manicured fingernail. "Yeah . . . 'Constellation will miss Saturday. Call her back, she can chat to-day!'" As she read, Galleria's voice twizzled into a Jamaican accent. "Ohhh, right," she said sheepishly. "I did this one as the Jamaican vibe I was feeling for the girls." Galleria started to move to a reggae beat. "Constellation will miss Saturday. Call her back, she can chat to-day! Chat-chat, giddy, giddy! Go, Mama, go! Boop! Boop!"

Dorothea danced along for a moment, smiling . . . but the smile quickly turned chilly. "So that's your excuse for making me look flaky with one of my best customers? Coming up with this . . . Cheetah chatter?" She shook her head and stomped to her office in the next room.

Just then, Galleria's father, Francobollo, waltzed into the room, singing opera at the top of his lungs.

"Papa!" Galleria cried, dashing over to him. "Just in time!"

Francobollo was a tall, lanky Italian man with a trim beard and a wide smile. He flipped a dish towel over his shoulder as he leaned over to look his daughter in the eye. "My chicken picata is waiting for the capers I asked you to bring home," he said in his heavy Italian accent.

Galleria blinked at him. "Capers," she said in a tiny voice. "Right." She swallowed hard. "My bad. My big bad."

Francobollo put his hands on either side of Galleria's face. "Do me a favor and bring this pretty head down out of the clouds and use it, please?"

"I am using my head," Galleria insisted. "When my plan jumps off, you'll be up to your ears in capers."

"And what plan might that be?" Dorothea asked from the doorway. She stepped back into the room and sat down. "I think I'd better have a seat, because this is going to be a very long story. Don't you think so, Papa?"

Galleria's father chuckled and went to stand behind his wife.

"First prize in the school talent show is time in a real recording studio," Galleria explained. "To make a demo like a pro, you know? Then we put that demo in some big willy hands, and it's ka-ching, ka-ching, bling, bling, bling!"

"I thought it was only bling-bling," Francobollo said. "Now there's three blings?"

"Fame and fortune. Just like that, huh?" Dorothea looked doubtful.

"Monique Twig, Electra Breeze," Galleria said, listing two well-known pop singers, "all talent show winners, all platinum. And Jackal Johnson went to Manhattan Magnet, too, way back in the nineties."

Dorothea lifted an eyebrow. "Oh, way back before the Internet, and all that, hmm?"

Galleria giggled and rolled her eyes. "Mom, he's not *that* old!" she insisted. "Cheetah Girls are next in line to win this thing. And when we do, we'll be needing buckets for the duckets when they rain down. Then I will cover you in ice. And we'll have 'yes, sir, no, sir' butlers and maids to do all the chores." Galleria waggled her eyebrows. "How do you like that plan?"

Reaching out, Dorothea pressed her daughter's hands between her own. "I love that you have a dream, honey. Your dreams and your plans are very important to us. But before we can get to maids and butlers and ice, we have to focus on some responsibility. So!" She leaned back in her chair. "Here's *my* plan: you are going to focus on real life and real chores, real, real soon." Dorothea dangled Toto's leash in front of Galleria.

"Okay," Galleria said sincerely. "Deal. I'll get it together. Come on, Caper," she added as she snapped Toto's leash to his collar. "Daddy needs Totos."

I can't wait until I have a maid to do this chore, Galleria thought as she hurried out the door. Then I can spend all of my time in the recording studio, where I belong!

In another part of town, Chanel hummed the lyrics to "Together" as she walked into the loft apartment she shared with her mother and brother. She hung her coat on a chair at the kitchen table, then walked over to the counter and grabbed a handful of cereal out of a box. That was when she noticed the pink feather boa lying on the counter. Frowning, Chanel picked it up . . . then spotted a shirt on the floor, and a skirt halfway down the hall. Chanel followed the trail of clothing to her bedroom, where clothes were flying out of her closet as though they were caught in a tornado.

"Looking for something, Mom?" Chanel asked, pulling off the red shirt that had just landed on her head.

"Found it," Juanita sang, salsa stepping through Chanel's room on her way to the bathroom mirror. "The *bomb* top to wear to dinner tonight."

"Mom, don't say 'bomb,'" Chanel corrected. "It's out. Say 'tight.'" Just then, she got a look at the clingy baby T-shirt Juanita had on. "As in, that top is too tight for anybody's *mother* to be wearing!" Chanel dumped the pile of clothes she had collected onto the floor and hurried over to her closet.

"*¿Y como fue la fiesta?*" Juanita asked as she peered into the bathroom mirror.

"It was cold," Chanel griped. "But the Cheetah Girls—" She sighed as she watched her mother arrange her blond hair in the mirror. "Ma, what about this?" Chanel asked, holding up a blouse. "It's cheetah-licious!"

"Ooh, now this *is* tight!" Juanita examined the blouse. "You're going to be my daughter, the fashion buyer."

"No, Ma!" Chanel backed out of the bathroom and flopped onto her bed. "I'm going to be your daughter the Cheetah Girl, remember?"

"Did you say something, *mija?*" Juanita called.

"Yeah, I said . . ." Oh, forget it, Chanel thought. She's not paying attention, anyway. "Another date with that French guy?"

"Excuse me," Juanita said from the doorway, planting her hands on her hips. "Luc is not just 'that French guy.' How would you like it if people called you 'that' Puerto Rican/Cuban/Dominican girl?"

"They *do*," Chanel insisted as she hauled herself over to the vanity. "That's who I am."

"No. No, no, no, no, no. I taught you that what matters is what's inside." Juanita leaned against the vanity and looked at her daughter. "And deep inside, Luc is very, very . . ." She paused, searching for the right word. "Rich."

"Dang, Mom," Chanel said. "When you say that, you sound like you like him just for his money."

"Good," Juanita replied. "Then I've made myself clear." Juanita's eyes twinkled. "No, just joking."

The front door buzzer rang.

"There he is," Juanita sang as she scurried into the kitchen for her bag. "All right, baby, you're going to lock up, okay? Pucci is staying at your dad's, so you don't have to worry about him."

"Ma—" Chanel said.

"I'm on celly, jelly."

"Ma, I want to talk to you—"

"Okay, listen, we'll talk later," Juanita said as she hurried toward the door. "I'm so late—"

❖ ❖ ❖ ❖ ❖ ❖ ❖ ❖ ❖ ❖ ❖ ❖ ❖ ❖ ❖ ❖ ❖

Chanel rolled her eyes as her mother yanked down the elevator gate and disappeared. She trudged to the kitchen and stuck her hand back into the box of cereal. "By the way, Mom, I hit a high C today with the Cheetah Girls," she said to herself. She couldn't help smiling at the memory. "Cheetah Girls!"

"Madrina still not home yet?" Galleria asked Chanel on the phone later that night. Galleria and Chanel called each other's mothers *Madrina*, or godmother. Dorothea and Juanita had been friends since the days when they were models together, way back before the girls were born.

"Nope," Chanel replied. She was lying across her bed, trying to study for her history test the next day, but she just couldn't seem to focus. "I guess Mr. Tycoon flew her to Paris for dinner."

"I'm always here for you, Chuchie. You know that," Galleria said.

Chanel smiled wryly. "Thanks, Bubbles."

That was her nickname for Galleria—because Galleria was always chewing gum.

"No problem. Hey, girl, listen to this." Galleria sang a few bars of the new song she'd been working on. From his cheetah-print doggy bed, Toto started to bark. Then he leaped up, stood on his hind legs, and began to dance around. "Chuchie! Toto likes it! Is that one a hit? Yes, it's a hit! Go, Toto. Go, Cheetahs!" she sang. "Win the talent show! We're going straight to the top!"

Chanel laughed. "Let's get through the tryouts first."

Galleria rolled her eyes. They had that talent show stitched.

She was sure of it.

3

"Hey, Chanel, how did that test go?" Dorinda asked as the Cheetah Girls walked down the hall of Manhattan Magnet School the next day.

Chanel winced. "Not great. Are you sure the Louisiana Purchase did not involve gumbo at any point?" she asked.

Aqua blinked at her. "Gumbo?"

"You can't drop your grades now, Chuchie," Galleria insisted. "I'm calling a Cheetah study session."

Chanel pouted.

"Hey, I'll walk you through the mystery of her-story," Aqua said, patting her on the back. "And you can walk me through your closet."

Chanel and Aqua slapped hands front and back, then gave a high five, curling their fingers like cheetah claws.

"Mackerel, we've spotted the wild Cheetah Girls doing their secret handshake," an Australian-sounding voice said. A very tall, very blond, very cute guy named Derek Hambone smiled as he did his best Crocodile Hunter impersonation for the Cheetahs. "What would they do if they were, say, the elephant girls?"

Derek's friend Mackerel laughed, and the two boys waved their arms like trunks and trumpeted.

"Basta pasta, Derek!" Galleria said coolly. "You too, Mackerel. You know, we call ourselves the Cheetah Girls because they are the fiercest and the fastest felines in the jungle. Let's bounce, girls."

Derek grinned as he and Mackerel followed the Cheetahs into the lunchroom.

"I'm trying to keep it lite FM with you,

Derek," Galleria told him, picking up a lunch tray. "Saving my energy for the talent show audition. Remember? Or are you throwing in the towel since you know you're gonna lose?" Galleria sat down at a table.

Derek leaned over the back of her chair. "See, that's what I need to talk to you about," he said. "Your little project auditions at three-fifteen, and we're at three-thirty. Can we switch times? Our setup takes time 'cause we have, you know, *real* instruments," he added snidely.

Galleria scoffed. "And help you?" She shook her head. "I don't think so."

"I have an orthodontist appointment and my mom will freak if I'm late," Mackerel confessed, blowing Derek's cool cover. He flashed a pleading look at Chanel.

"Let them have our slot," Chanel said.

Everyone turned to stare at her.

"Mrs. Almanac wants to talk to me about my history test," Chanel added quickly.

Galleria sighed. "I don't like last-minute changes. How's everybody else?"

Aqua shrugged, sipping her juice.

"It's cutting it a little tight for me," Dorinda admitted, "but . . ."

"Where do you have to be all the time, girl?" Galleria asked, frowning.

"Nowhere," Dorinda said quickly. "I'm here. Don't worry, I'm fine."

"Okay, Hambone," Galleria told Derek. "Whatever. Just know that you can audition five times, you're still going to lose."

"Keep believing, freshman," Derek said. "I respect that." He leaned closer to Galleria. "You know you're still my boo," he murmured in her ear.

The Cheetah Girls squawked as the boys walked away.

"He is trying so hard not to like you," Dorinda said to Galleria.

"And maybe now would be a good time to point out that he is extra-specially cheetah-licious!" Aqua added, clapping her hands as the girls cracked up.

"It's a trick," Galleria said impatiently. "Every time he bats those long eyelashes, he's trying to bring the hammer down on our success! Don't fall for it."

At that moment, Derek and Mackerel turned to look over their shoulders and walked into a guy with a plateful of salad. A minute later, they were flat on the floor in a lettuce avalanche. The cafeteria erupted into hoots of laughter.

"He even makes embarrassing stuff look really, really cute," Aqua said, giggling. "And," she added, leaning across the table, "he wants you to be his boo."

The Cheetahs laughed.

Galleria frowned, but she was trying hard to ignore the little flutter in her heart. "He'll be the one crying boo-hoo when we win the talent show," she grumbled.

But she couldn't stop herself from sneaking another look at Derek. She had to admit that Aqua had a point—he *was* cheetah-licious. Even if he was a jerk.

4

❀ ❀ ❀ ❀ ❀ ❀ ❀ ❀ ❀ ❀ ❀ ❀ ❀ ❀ ❀ ❀ ❀ ❀

"May the growl power of all the fabulous divas who came before us be with us now," Chanel said as the Cheetahs huddled up before their audition. They were all wearing white outfits, accented with cheetah spots. "May we use our hearts, our brains, and our courage to help us reach our cheetah-licious potential, right here, right now."

The Cheetah girls exchanged a four-way handshake. "Cheetahs!" they cried.

It was on.

Pucci ran the lights as the Cheetah's music started. Just then, a tall figure disguised in a head scarf and dark glasses snuck into the auditorium, carrying a fluffy white dog. It was Dorothea. She spotted another figure in a head scarf and dark glasses—Juanita—and sat down beside her.

A dance beat bounced through the auditorium as the Cheetahs started to sing and move through their choreography.

In the audience, Juanita and Dorothea exchanged looks. Their daughters were good—really, really good. And they weren't the only ones who thought so. Midway through the song, Toto bolted out of Dorothea's lap and galloped toward the stage before she could stop him. He raced toward the Cheetah Girls and stood on his hind legs, dancing, as the girls finished their song.

The moms burst into applause as the song ended. "Brava!" Dorothea shouted. "Brava, divas!"

"So, Drinka," Galleria called from the stage. "Are we in?"

The only response was a snuffling sound.

"Drinka?" Aqua asked. "Drinka, are you still there?"

There was a loud honk as Drinka blew her nose.

"Drinka! Were we that bad?" Chanel asked.

"Yes," Pucci called. "Tell them," he said, looking over his shoulder at the teacher. "They can take it."

"I'm all right," Drinka said, squeezing her hankie. "I will survive. It's just that when I see you girls, I see myself." Drinka stood and walked down the center aisle toward them. She was wearing a loose, glittery top, gold satin pants, and crystal earrings—her usual disco diva style. "Not myself now as a lowly high school arts teacher," she went on. I mean, Drinka Champagne, 1977, top of the charts! I had a hit!" Drinka burst into song. "*Champagne bubbles of love! Ooh-ooh! That's what I'm dreaming of—*"

"Drinka. Drinka," Galleria interrupted. "Cool down that disco fever. Are we in the show?"

"Oh, you girls," Drinka said, waving her hankie at them. "I feel like you're little Drinka clones. Galleria, when I look at you, I see a biracial, hip-hopping version of me. And Chanel, when I look at you, honey, I see a hot-Latin-spicy version of me. And Aqua, when I look at you, I see myself as if I was from the sassy South. And Dorinda is me if I was—"

"If you were what?" Dorinda asked defensively. "Go ahead and say it. Everyone else does. 'Dorinda is like me if I was shrimpy and white.'"

Drinka shrugged. "I was going to say 'able to dance.'"

The Cheetah Girls dissolved into giggles.

"Drinka, we just want to know if we're in," Galleria said.

"Oh, yes, honey," Drinka replied. "You are in."

Squeals of Cheetah delight rang through the auditorium.

"But, Drinka," Chanel asked, "do we actually have a chance of winning?"

"Oh, yes, yes, yes," Drinka insisted. "Don't worry. I'll work with you like I did with Electra Breeze."

"Or maybe I'll work with them," said a voice from the back of the auditorium. A tall man with spiked blond hair and dark sunglasses emerged from the shadows.

Galleria shrieked. "Jackal Johnson?"

"You were here?" Dorinda cried as the music producer walked toward the stage, followed by a dreadlocked man in a suit and two large bodyguards. "Watching us?"

"My most famous student," Drinka said as she gave Jackal a kiss on the cheek. "You look fabulous! What are you doing here?"

"Well, I see the 'talent show' banner outside and I want to be back walking the halls." Jackal flashed a super-white grin. "I still keep my hand in the community."

"The Jackal keeps it real," said the guy with the dreadlocks. "Finger on the pulse."

"And I haven't seen this much talent on that stage since my graduation," Jackal said, nodding toward the Cheetah Girls, who giggled.

"The Cheetah Girls are my latest project," Drinka said.

"You always could spot talent, Drinka,"

Jackal said. "But now I'd like to talk to you ladies about the next step in your career."

"Jackal Johnson wants to work with us!" Chanel gasped.

"See, I'm looking for the next big thing," Jackal explained, "and I think that thing just might have spots."

The Cheetah Girls screeched in excitement.

But two people in the auditorium weren't quite as thrilled. "Let's get down there," Dorothea said to Juanita. A moment later, the two moms were hustling toward the stage.

Just then, Pucci stepped forward and held out a business card to Jackal. "Jackal, when you're ready to talk dollars and cents, my card. The Cheetah Girls' manager, Kid Salsa."

"Pucci!" Aqua cried, yanking him away.

"Get your brother out of here," Galleria said to Chanel.

Handing Toto to Aqua, Galleria stepped forward. "Hello, Jackal Johnson," she said, extending her hand. "My name is Galleria Garibaldi. I wrote 'Cinderella,' and I'm the founder of the Cheetah Girls."

The other members of the group exchanged looks. *The founder?*

"Which I hope to record for you," Galleria went on, "in the near future."

"Excellent," Jackal said. "So let's set something up. Schedule?" He snapped his fingers, and Dreadlocks handed him a Palm Pilot.

"Hold on," Dorothea interrupted suddenly. "I'm Dorothea Garibaldi, and there's a misunderstanding here. Singing is just a fun sideline for our girls. They're not professionals."

"*Mom*," Galleria said through clenched teeth, "this is Jackal Johnson. He's one of the biggest record producers of my time, Mother."

Dorothea lifted her eyebrows and looked at Jackal. "Let's see . . . eight Grammys, twenty million-dollar label deal, multipicture movie deal, four houses, seven cars . . . and he's allergic to dogs."

"Nice work," Jackal told her, clearly impressed.

"I read." Dorothea flashed her daughter a look, then turned back to Jackal. "It's so nice to have met you, Mr. . . ."

"Jackal Johnson."

"Yes, Jackal Johnson," Dorothea repeated. "Yes, of course." She shook his hand, then turned and stalked away.

"Girls, come on," Juanita said. "I'm going to take us all out to eat. Okay? Get your stuff."

Reluctantly, the Cheetahs turned and trudged backstage. Galleria hesitated. This was her big chance, and she couldn't bear to let it go.

"Here's my card," Jackal told her in a low voice. "Just in case. Your mom's no joke."

"No," Galleria said sadly. "None. Never. Bye, Mr. Johnson."

5

"Thanks for dropping me off," Dorinda said to Galleria and her mom. "I live right here." The cab they were riding in pulled up in front of an elegant building where a doorman stood at attention in a cap and cape.

"Watch the cars," Dorothea cautioned as Dorinda stepped out of the taxi and shut the door behind her.

Galleria couldn't even muster a good-bye.

"She seems like a nice girl." Dorothea watched Dorinda walk toward the building. "What are her parents like?"

Galleria sat staring straight ahead. "She has a little sister, but that's all we know. Her parents aren't always up in her thing. They *trust* her," she added meaningfully.

"You got in the talent show," Dorothea replied. "Please don't spoil this day because you didn't get everything you wanted. At this rate, you're headed straight to your room."

Galleria had to fight back tears. She knew there wasn't any point in arguing with her mother.

They sat in silence for the rest of the cab ride, but by the time they got home, Galleria just couldn't hold it in any longer. "Mom, Jackal Johnson liked my song!" she wailed as she burst into the living room, where her father was sitting. "That was our big chance. Don't you think we're talented?"

"Of course, sweetheart, you're incredibly talented. You know I think that," Dorothea said, adjusting the leopard-print scarf that hung around her shoulders. "You'll be just as talented *after* college."

"One CD and I could pay for college fifty times over!" Galleria shouted.

"But you won't have time to study,"

Dorothea snapped, "so you won't have the grades to get in. And that, my dear, is called a paradox."

"Colleges don't just look at grades," Galleria pointed out. "Plus, not everybody even goes to college, you know."

"Galleria, you're not helping yourself here," Francobollo said.

"Daddy, tell her," Galleria begged. "I'm not a knucklehead!"

"Calm down, honey," Francobollo said. "You know, you have to listen to your mother's advice."

"The bottom line is, you're too young, Galleria." Dorothea's voice trembled with emotion. "I've been there. I've seen what happens when a young girl is under pressure and can't handle it."

"Silly people do silly things no matter what age they are! I get good grades, Mom," Galleria pleaded. "I spend more time on my homework than my hair. I set my mind to something and I almost get there and you stand in the way. What's the point of eating your vegetables if you don't ever get any dessert?"

Dorothea glared at her daughter. "Strong bones and teeth."

Francobollo gave Galleria a warning look, and then followed Dorothea, who had just stormed out of the room. Galleria flung herself onto her bed and screamed into her cheetah-print pillow. This was just so unfair!

"It's not fair that we can't talk to Jackal, Mom," Chanel griped as she stood beside her mother at the bathroom mirror. They wore matching blue bathrobes and were both smearing a goopy cleansing mask on their faces.

"Honey, I think Dorothea's instincts are right on this one," Juanita said as she surveyed her face in the mirror. "You don't need to be working with that Jackal. With all that platinum and those big chains. *Tan* tacky!"

"Mom, it doesn't matter how he dresses!" Chanel exclaimed.

"He's not like the men from Paris," Juanita huffed. "Luc is always on point."

Chanel crossed her eyes in frustration. "Mom, can you forget Luc for just one half a second? I'm really upset, here!"

A slow smile spread across Juanita's lips. "And I know what will cheer you up."

"You're going to talk to Madrina and change her mind?" Chanel guessed.

"Nope. Shopping!" Juanita said brightly. "You and me. Shopping."

"Okay. *Then* you'll talk to Madrina?" Chanel asked hopefully.

"Yes. Now, I have to ask you . . ." Juanita wrapped her arm around her daughter. "What do you think about Paris?"

"What—Luc wants you to visit?"

"To visit . . ." Juanita's smile sparkled in the mirror. "To live . . ."

Chanel shrugged off her mother's arm. "Whoa—*what*?" Just then, the phone rang. Chanel ran into the other room to answer it. "Hello? Hold on, Bubbles . . ." She turned back to face her mother. "To *live*?"

"Promise me you'll think about it," Juanita said from the doorway.

"I'm thinking, all right!" Chanel groaned. "Bubbles, thank goodness it's you," she said into the phone. "My life is over!"

But Galleria had her own problems. "She won't even let me call Jackal," she griped as she paced around her room. "She used every excuse in the book to ruin our lives. But this is not over. We're not dropping all our hard work."

"Juanita's talking about moving to Paree with Mr. Tycoon!" Chanel wailed.

"Didn't they see us tonight?" Galleria demanded as she flopped into her desk chair. "Don't they know our futures are right here?"

"It's sick," Chanel agreed. "She dangled a shopping trip in my face, then lowered the boom."

"Tell her no chance, no dance. Wait," Galleria said, thinking fast. "Take the shopping trip first."

"Galleria—" Francobollo suddenly walked back into his daughter's room. "Your mother and I . . ." Francobollo gestured behind himself, and then noticed that his wife wasn't there. "'Scuse," he said, ducking back through the door.

"Girl, hold on a second," Galleria said into the receiver, "something's about to happen."

A moment later, Francobollo reappeared, shoving Dorothea before him.

Dorothea sighed. "Your father thinks this might be a good experience for you," she said reluctantly. "So you can call that record producer person—"

With a squeal of delight, Galleria threw her arms around her mother. "Thank you! Thank you! Thank you!"

"But there are conditions," Dorothea warned.

Galleria rolled her eyes and headed back to her desk chair. "I'd better sit down for this."

"First, I'm going with you to the meeting," Dorothea explained. "And second, if I don't like what I see, we're gone. And number three—"

"Number three," Francobollo put in, wrapping his arms around his wife, "she promises to keep an open mind."

Dorothea laughed, and Francobollo winked at Galleria as he pulled her mother out the door. Galleria winked back. I should have known Papa would stand up for me! Galleria thought. "Chuchie, yes!" Galleria whispered into the phone, "They're going to let me call Jackal! Dad comes through for me again!"

"Wow!" Chanel said. "We're gonna have our penthouse soon!"

"Today has been . . ." Galleria searched her brain for the perfect word, "Cheetah crazy!"

"Yeah," Chanel agreed. She paused. Now that they had one problem solved, there was something she needed to bring up with her best friend. "You were definitely a little loco tonight. Since when are you the 'founder' of the Cheetah Girls?"

Galleria frowned. "What?"

"That's what you told Jackal." Chanel's voice took on a high-pitched, super-breathy tone and she crossed her eyes as she imitated Galleria. "'I wrote "Cinderella" and I'm the founder of the Cheetah Girls,' and yadda, yadda . . ."

"You know I didn't mean it like that, Chuchie," Galleria said. "I wanted to jump in there before my mother did. You know I'll do whatever's clever to keep the Cheetah Girls on the prowl."

Chanel sighed. She knew her friend was telling the truth—even if she *had* been out of line. Galleria really would do whatever it took to keep the Cheetah Girls stalking the jiggy jungle.

And that was a good thing, right?

6

"Thanks very much," Galleria chirped into her cell phone during lunch at school the next day. "We will be awaiting your call. Have a wonderful day." She flipped her phone closed and grinned at the other Cheetahs. "She'll call me back with a time on Friday. We're going to meet with Jackal Johnson!"

"Hey," Derek said as he and Mackerel walked over to the Cheetahs' table. "It's all over school about your fifteen minutes of Jackal fame." Derek slipped into the seat next to Galleria and grinned at her.

"Yes, well," Galleria said nonchalantly, "we're very fortunate."

"Well, while you were crossing paws with Jackal Johnson, we rushed off to a lecture by the great Wynton Marsalis." Derek smiled smugly.

"We actually couldn't afford tickets," Mackerel admitted from his place next to Chanel, "so we drank mochaccinos across the street. Well, I had hot chocolate—"

"Wynton came in," Derek interjected. "He sat two tables from us. We exchanged ideas."

Mackerel gave Derek a look. "Nah, man. You handed him a sugar packet."

"Busted!" Aqua said as the other Cheetahs cracked up.

"Hey, Cheetahs!" A pretty Asian girl named Julie bounced over to their table. "Can you guys come by the newspaper office for an interview? That Jackal story is front page!"

"Sure!" Galleria said, flashing a bright smile. "Always down for the photo op!"

"My boy handed Marsalis a sugar packet last night," Mackerel told Julie, gesturing toward Derek. "We can't get no ink?" With that,

Derek and Mackerel stood up and walked off.

"He is just so fine," Aqua said through bites of turkey burger as she watched the boys walk away.

"Are you crazy?" Galleria demanded. "If he can't respect my art, he can't have my heart. Oooh. Lyric moment." She scribbled the words in her notebook.

"What-*ever*," Aqua said, popping a mini éclair into her mouth. "We're on the front page," she garbled with her mouth full. She and Dorinda exchanged the Cheetah paw shake.

Galleria stared at them. "Hold it down! Now that we're going to be stars, we need to start acting like it."

"And how's that?" Aqua asked, her mouth still full of chocolate pastry.

Galleria sighed. "Stars don't talk with their mouths full." She reached over and picked a bottle of red pepper sauce off of Aqua's tray. "And they don't carry bottles of Hot Papa sauce around in their purses."

"Stars that know good food do," Aqua insisted, still chewing. "I love New York, but y'all don't know nothing about spicing some food. I take a little Texas wherever I go, believe that."

"Well, Aqua, I have a problem with your table manners. You'd better stash the sauce when Jackal is around." Reaching into her bag, Galleria slipped on a pair of sunglasses with cheetah-print rims, then stood up and walked away.

Aqua stared after her. "She took my hot sauce," Aqua complained.

"Guys, she's right," Chanel said, handing Aqua a napkin. "Looks do count."

Chanel had to back up her friend on this one. Galleria was right . . . even if she had been kind of rude.

That afternoon, at the youth center, Dorinda had just finished her mopping when she saw her dance instructor place a sign on the front desk.

"Closed on Saturday!" Dorinda read.

"We've rented the space to the Gold Medal Crew video people for their auditions," Dana explained.

"But I need credit for working those hours, Dana," Dorinda said, her eyes wide. "How am I going to pay for my lessons?"

Dana thought for a moment. "Help me run the auditions, and I'll credit you for two weeks of lessons," she said.

"Really?" Dorinda grinned. Help run the auditions for the Gold Medal Crew? They were the hottest hip-hop dance troupe in the country!

One thing was for sure—it definitely beat mopping.

Later that night, Galleria sat at her keyboard in her bedroom, working on her new song for the Cheetah Girls, "Girl Power."

"How do you like that, Toto?" she asked after she'd sung a few lines.

With a happy bark, Toto leaped onto Galleria's lap.

"I like it, too," Galleria said, patting Toto's

fur. "It's cheetah-licious. This is going to be our demo. This is taking us to the top. I'm ready for Jackal." She sighed. "I hope everybody else is."

7

Galleria's heart pounded as she sat in the back of the cab the next morning, nervously ticking off a mental list of everything she wanted to say to Jackal. I just want this meeting to be perfect, she thought. Even the slightest mistake could kill our chances.

"If Dorinda is sitting there in those same clothes she wears every day, I think I'm going to scream," Galleria said out loud.

Dorothea glanced out the window at the traffic that was stopped dead all around them. They had only gone three blocks in the past ten minutes, and they were working on being seriously late to the meeting. "Do you want to walk?" she asked her daughter.

Galleria looked down at her footwear. She had on supercool spike-heeled boots. Great for looking. Bad for walking.

Dorothea sighed. "Always travel in comfortable shoes. Bring heels in a bag and slip them on right before. I told you that."

"Right, Mom, right," Galleria said. She knew better—but she'd had so many other things on her mind.

"You know what, sweetheart, if this Jackal guy wants just one penny of you girls' money, then he's not for real," Dorothea said.

"Mom!" Galleria wailed.

"I know these impresario types," Dorothea insisted. "The head of my modeling agency was just like that, and—"

"We're lucky to even be in the office with Jackal Johnson!" Galleria insisted. "Please don't 'Mom' it to death. Please." Galleria craned her neck to look out the front windshield. The traffic still wasn't moving, despite the chorus of horns blaring around them.

"Sweetheart, let me give you just one more piece of advice," Dorothea said. "Make the meeting. Soak your feet later."

Galleria looked at her mom. Finally, she had a good point.

A moment later, Galleria was trotting after her mother, who *had* worn comfortable shoes and was striding down the sidewalk at light speed. "Mom, slow down!" Galleria called. "Sweat rings! Bad first impression to stink up the place."

Dorothea didn't slacken her pace, and Galleria hobbled after her. I guess I'll try not to worry about the sweat rings, she thought. Maybe nobody will notice.

Meanwhile, the other Cheetah Girls were waiting in the lobby of Def Duck Records, getting nervous.

"What time is it?" Chanel asked for the thousandth time.

"Quarter past time to be on time," Aqua growled.

"Where is she?" Dorinda griped.

Just then, Jackal strode into the room. "There they are," he said warmly, "my Cheetah Girls!"

"Galleria's running a little late, Mr. Johnson," Chanel said timidly.

"Number one," Jackal said as he took off his blue-tinted shades, "Mr. Johnson is my father's name. Call me Jackal."

The Cheetah Girls giggled.

"Let's take the tour of your new home while we wait for the other divette to make her entrance," Jackal suggested.

The girls looked at each other excitedly. A tour of Def Duck records?

Jackal took them all over the Def Duck offices, introducing them to marketing people, showing them the studios, and even buying them a snack at the cafeteria. Jackal didn't act like he was the "boss," or anything. He treated the Cheetah Girls like they were important. He's so friendly and nice, Chanel thought. We are so incredibly lucky!

"I'm all about the South!" Jackal said to Aqua as he led the Cheetahs back into the lobby. "Spent every summer at my grand-father's place in Dallas."

"Don't mess with Texas," Aqua and Jackal said together.

Just then, Galleria and Dorothea strode through the front door.

"Sorry I'm late, everybody," Galleria said.

A pungent odor wafted past Chanel's nose. She looked down at Galleria's feet. Oh, no! Her best friend had tracked in a little surprise on the sole of her shoe. One by one, the other Cheetahs' noses wrinkled. So did Jackal's. Looking around, Chanel could tell that everyone was smelling what she was smelling . . . everyone *except* for Galleria.

"Jackal, you wouldn't believe the traffic," Galleria went on.

Chanel hurried over to her best friend. "Bubbles, can I see you for a second?" she asked in a low voice.

"Later, Chanel," Galleria said, frowning slightly. "Jackal's time is valuable. I want to get started. I just hope I haven't missed any-thing."

"Nope," Jackal said with a tiny smile. "Smells like you brought it all with you."

Confusion flickered across Galleria's face, and her mother leaned over and whispered in her ear.

The change in Galleria's expression from disbelief to horror was so hysterical that Chanel actually had to bite her lip to keep from laughing. She grabbed Galleria's hand and led her—hopping on her dog-poop-free foot—down the hall toward the ladies' room.

"It's okay now, Galleria," Chanel said as she swiped at her friend's shoe with a rag the cleaning staff had loaned them.

"It's not okay, Chuchie!" Galleria wailed from her seat on the bathroom counter. "We have the most spectaculous meeting of our careers, and I march in and make fudgy feet all over the room. Everybody got my whiff today! He's never going to work with us now!"

"Galleria, the Cheetah Girls is four people," Chanel reminded her as she slid the boot back on to Galleria's foot.

"I know, I know. But I've got to pull it together. Enough with the powder puff. It's showtime, baby. When you boil it down, that's what being the leader is all about." Galleria hopped off the counter and patted Chanel on the head. "Thanks for having my back, Chuchie. You're the one."

The leader? Chanel glared after her friend and tossed the rag in the sink.

Galleria's feet weren't the only thing that was stinky around here.

"Hey!" Jackal said as Galleria walked into the studio where he was standing with the other Cheetahs and Dorothea. "Come on over here, my little Pooptracker!"

Dorinda and Aqua cracked up. Galleria shot them a deadly glare.

"You all good again?" Jackal asked.

"I'm fine," Galleria said in her most professional voice. "So, maybe we should get down to business."

"Business? The deal is done." Jackal grinned and held up a small red bottle. "Aqua pulled out a bottle of Hot Papa hot sauce, and I was sold."

Galleria's eyebrows flew up. "Really? What can I say?"

Aqua grinned. "Nothing!" she replied.

Reaching into her bag, Galleria pulled out a CD. "Well, I brought our new song with me, so you can look at it. My dog Toto says it's a hit."

"Oh, that's nice," Jackal said. He took the CD, but he barely even glanced at it before reaching for a folder. "And I've got some paperwork for the Mama-cheetah. Standard agreement."

Dorothea flipped open the folder and clicked her pen. Red ink flew across the page as she made notes, added phrases, and crossed out entire sections. "Standard revisions," she said to Jackal. "And then my lawyer will weigh in, and—"

"Mom," Galleria warned, flashing her mother a glare.

"Chuchie, it's Gucci . . . line one,"
Galleria said.

"May we use our hearts, our brains, and our
courage to help us reach our cheetah-licious
potential, right here, right now," Chanel said.

"Make the meeting. Soak your feet later," Dorothea said.

"He's never going to work with us now!" Galleria wailed.

"Galleria is making it hard to wear Cheetah spots," Dorinda said.

"I knew it was too good to be true," Chanel grumbled.

"I'm a foster child," Dorinda told Chanel.

"Friends help friends make their dreams come true, right?" Galleria said.

"How does it look?" Dorinda asked.

"Girl Power!" the Cheetah Girls sang.

"We can't trust you anymore,"
Chanel told Galleria.

"The Cheetahs are extinct,"
Galleria admitted.

"I was thinking that Toto and I could go down to the talent show and show Drinka some support," Galleria said.

"Okay, 'Together,'" Dorinda said.

"Girl, we didn't take that deal,"
Aqua said.

"Tell him the Cheetah Girls are
unavailable," Galleria said.

"Okey-dokey," Jackal said, clapping his hands. "Here's my checklist: number one, record a bumpin' demo. Number Two, have the record people fall in love with it. Three, make millions. So, who's down for that?" Jackal asked.

The Cheetahs let out an excited squeal.

"So, exactly how much time is it going to take to make this 'bumpin' demo'?" Dorothea asked.

"Well, we don't want to pull you girls out of school, so—schedule?" The man with the dreadlocks handed Jackal his Palm Pilot. "Tuesday night, we learn the song. Run it Wednesday, Thursday, Friday nights. Rest up and on Saturday, we lay down some tracks."

"Less than a week?" Dorothea demanded. "These girls need more than a week to rehearse, then they need time to make it their own . . ."

"Mom, I wrote the song," Galleria put in. "We know the song."

"You've got to grab each voice," Dorothea

continued, ticking off on her fingers, "digitize each track in real time . . . It's a lot to do."

"Down, down, Mama-cheetah," Jackal teased. "Remember, this is a teensy-weensy little demo. Not a soundtrack album. All I need is one clean take, then the bells and whistles happen right here. So . . . Saturday."

"Oh!" Chanel said suddenly. "Our school talent show."

Galleria smiled. "Don't even worry about that. We'll be here," she told Jackal.

"That's what I like to hear," Jackal said.

Chanel frowned. So the talent show is off? she thought. Just because Galleria said so? It was starting to sound like Galleria had forgotten that there was more than one cheetah in the jungle.

"Fresh! Bam! Off the Cheetah-meter!" Galleria said as the Cheetahs walked out of Def Duck Records.

Chanel looked skeptical. "And now the talent show is down the drain?"

"Hey, don't worry about it," Galleria said,

holding up her hand. "Drinka will understand."

"I hope you know you're not singing a note
until my lawyer looks this over thoroughly,"
Dorothea said, holding up the paperwork.

"Mom," Galleria scoffed, "things were different back in your day. If Jackal thinks we're
ready, we must be ready!"

"My day, your day," Dorothea replied, "a
snake is still a snake."

Galleria huffed. That was just like her mom
to try to ruin her dreams. But she wasn't
going to let anyone stop her now. She was too
close.

8

* * * * * * * * * * * * * * * * * * *

"This week is crazy, Julie," Galleria said to the school newspaper editor as she handed her a press packet she had worked up for the Cheetah Girls. "But you'll get time with all the Cheetah Girls. We trust you to get our story right, but I need photo sign-off, you understand. And I promise, you will be short-listed when the movie deal comes along. And it will."

Julie just stared at her. Lately, Galleria had been spending all of her time talking Cheetah. She spent every lunch period telling anyone who would listen about their meeting with Jackal. In fact, she was starting to drive people a little crazy. . . .

"What's the story?" Chanel asked as Aqua and Dorinda led her to a wall in the school hallway that was papered with orange flyers.

"Not *our* story," Aqua corrected. "Galleria's. And it's written all over the walls." Aqua ripped down a flyer and handed it to Chanel.

"'Sick of Cheetahs?'" Chanel read aloud. "'Us, too! Click on Chompchectah dot com!'" She looked up at her friends and flipped the flyer to the ground. "We have a bashing site? It's really kind of funny that people are so jealous."

"Jealous?" Dorinda flashed her a get-over-yourself look. "You don't get it, do you? Galleria's over the top."

"I know she's tough," Chanel admitted. "She's proud of what we're doing. We should be, too. If you don't believe, nobody else will, and—"

"Save it for your book, Chanel," Dorinda cracked. "We live here. We have to go to school here. She's making it very hard to wear Cheetah spots."

"Look, all I'm saying is that someone needs

to talk to her," Aqua added. "And when I say someone, I mean *you*."

Chanel sighed. "I will," she said finally. "I will talk to her." It was becoming clear that somebody had to. But she wasn't looking forward to it. "When the time is right," she added quietly to herself.

"All right, girls," Drinka said, turning toward the Cheetahs, who were sitting behind her. The Manhattan Magnet auditorium was packed with kids waiting to rehearse for the talent show. "Let's get this rehearsal going."

"Actually, Drinka, I think we should work on my new song first," Galleria said as she and the other girls headed toward the stage.

Chanel turned to listen. It sounded like Galleria was making a decision for the group—again.

"No!" Drinka exclaimed. "Honey, you've got to boogie oogie oogie through your number for the talent show."

"Drinka," Galleria said, giving the teacher a

tight little smile, "you know we met with Jackal on Monday, right?"

"Mmm-hmm." Drinka nodded. "Heard it through the grapevine."

"Well," Galleria said, "he wants us in the studio to record our new song . . . on Saturday."

Derek nearly fell out of his chair. "You're not doing the talent show?" he asked as he rushed down the steps to face Galleria.

"Well, I'm going to try my best to be there," Galleria said quickly. "But you know how these things go, Drinka."

Drinka frowned. "Nope. Tell me how these things go."

"Wait a second, Drinka." Galleria flashed her best grin. "I thought you'd be happy for us. You hooked us up in the first place. Jackal's just there to get our stuff out there. It's like we already won the talent show, isn't it? Right?"

Drinka smiled back, but it was a smile dripping with sarcasm. "No," she said brightly, "not really. But I guess you just don't see that."

"Opportunity is knocking, Drinka," Galleria said, as though she was talking to a slow-witted child. "We can't miss a chance like this. You know better than I do that when it's gone, you can't get it back."

Chanel sucked in her breath. Galleria had really gone too far this time. That was down-right rude.

But Drinka didn't lose her cool. "You know what? I don't have much but this school, you kids, and my word. But that's me. I always keep my word. Come on, boys," she told Mackerel and Derek. "You're up."

Drinka led the boys toward the stage.

"Yo," Chanel said to Galleria, once Drinka was out of earshot. "That was pretty harsh."

"Okay, fine," Galleria told her. "You call Jackal and tell him, 'Sorry, can't tour this summer, we're rooty-poot and we've got a talent show.'"

"Well are we going to do it or not?" Dorinda demanded. "'Cause I got somewhere to be."

"Go ahead, Dorinda," Galleria said off-handedly, clutching her Cheetah Girls folder against her chest. "We're going to work on music. And since you mostly just dance—"

Dorinda's expression darkened. "Right," she said in a dangerous voice. "That's what I mostly do."

"Oh, and take these with you." Galleria dug in her bag, and came up with a stack of magazine clippings. "I got you these cute little clippings of outfits, which you can probably put together and hook it up for the next time we see Jackal."

With a snort, Dorinda turned away.

"Hey, Do," Galleria said, thrusting the pictures at her. "Take it. Because it's not optional."

Dorinda snatched the papers out of Galleria's hand with narrowed eyes. "And where do you go for your personality makeover?" she demanded. "Because, uh, I forgot."

"Don't go on the wack-attack, Do," Galleria warned. "We love you, but you can't look torn up and janky the next time we see Jackal."

"*We?*" Chanel whispered to Aqua.

"Torn up?" Dorinda demanded. "How's this for torn up?" She ripped the pictures into little pieces and stormed away.

Galleria shrugged. "Sometimes people just don't see how they're coming off to others," she said, turning to Chanel and Aqua. "She'll thank me in the long run."

"Miss Chanel," Aqua said sternly, as Galleria walked off, "the time is now."

Chanel swallowed hard. She knew she needed to talk to Galleria. But it just wasn't that easy.

9

"Okay, let's go!" André Miller, the director of the Gold Medal Crew, called as he herded the dancers to the center of the floor for the audition. "It's supposed to look fun. Lots of energy. Okay, let me get the first group."

Dorinda skipped to the front. Dana had already taught her the combination—she was just there to lead the auditioning dancers in case they forgot the steps. She smiled as she danced—the Gold Medal Crew's choreography was tight, and she was all over it.

"Don't get lost!" André called to one of the dancers, and Dorinda turned up the energy so the dancer would have someone to follow.

Dorinda shouted encouragement to the other dancers, and even added in a no-handed cartwheel in the middle of a combination, to keep it fresh.

"Who's that?" André asked Dana as he watched Dorinda lead the other dancers.

Dana grinned. "That's Dorinda."

"Okay, let's stop the music!" André called. The dancers stopped, and Dorinda trotted over to the corner for her bag and towel.

"Very nice, very nice," André said. "Guys, just hang out for a second—I'll be with you in a minute." André followed Dorinda to the corner. "Hey, Dorinda," he said. "You were working hard out there. You looked great."

Dorinda smiled up at him. "I'm glad I could help."

"Listen," André told her, "there are several parts in the stage show you would be perfect for. Think about coming on tour with us this summer."

"Me?" Dorinda repeated. "On tour? With the Gold Medal Crew?"

André nodded. "Ten weeks. There's a

couple of kids in the show. It's like summer camp, but you get paid."

"Wait—" Dorinda wasn't sure she'd heard that right. Get paid? To tour with the Gold Medal Crew? It was too good to be true!

"You dance like a pro," André said with a smile, "you get paid like a pro. Have your parents take a look at this." He handed Dorinda a permission form. "If they say yes, fill it out and return it to me."

Dorinda looked down at the paperwork. "My parents?" she asked. "Okay. All right. I'll get back to you." She grinned as she danced out of the youth center. "Oh man!" she said out loud.

How many dreams could come true in one week?

"Mom!" Chanel called as she stepped out of the elevator and into her apartment. "Let's go! I'm feeling shoe shoppy!" There was no answer. Just then, Chanel's eyes fell on a note that was propped up on a bottle of vinegar. Juanita's platinum credit card lay next to it. "I knew it was too good to be true," Chanel grumbled. "'Luc surprised me with tickets to a Broadway show,'" she read aloud, "'so I couldn't say no. But take my card and have a good time. Get something we both can wear and look tight. Love, Mommie.'" Putting the note down in disgust, Chanel grabbed a glass and poured herself some tap water. "'We need to spend more time together,'" she mimicked. "Yeah, right."

The phone rang.

"Nobody's home," Chanel told the phone. "Nobody's *ever* home!"

"Hey, we're not here," Juanita's voice said on the answering machine. "Leave your name and number after the beep."

"Juanita!" a super-chirpy voice blared through the machine. "Gail from Moving On Realtors. If you still want to put your apartment up for sale, give a shout, we'll do an open house!"

Chanel picked up the receiver just as Gail hung up. "Here's a shout for you!" Chanel screeched at the dial tone. "Cancel that order

and send it back special delivery. Nobody's moving out, *claro*? *Gracias!*"

Grabbing the platinum credit card, Chanel stormed toward the door. "Oh, yeah," she snarled to herself. "I'll have a good time."

10

❀❀❀❀❀❀❀❀❀❀❀❀❀❀❀❀❀❀❀❀❀❀

Chanel walked up to the fancy building, struggling with the weight of the bags in her hands. She had just done some shopping that was ten kinds of crazy, and she couldn't wait to show Dorinda what she had bought. After all, Chanel felt kind of bad that Galleria had gone completely loco about Dorinda's clothes. Maybe all Do needed was a little inspiration. They could compare outfits and pull some stuff out of Dorinda's closet. . . .

"Hello," Chanel said to the doorman as she walked up to Dorinda's building. "The Thomases, please?"

The doorman shook his head and held out

his arm to keep Chanel from walking in. "There are no Thomases here."

"Really?" Chanel checked the address—she was sure that she had dropped Dorinda off once or twice in front of this building. "Dorinda Thomas? About this tall. Always has a dance bag with her?"

"Oh, her!" The doorman gestured toward the side of the building. "Around to the alley, down the stairs. Superintendent's apartment."

"Alley?" Chanel murmured as she followed the doorman's directions. Pushing open an iron gate, she walked into a dim alley. She found a sign that said RING FOR SUPERINTEN-DENT, MR. BOSCO, so she pressed the button to the left. After a moment, the door swung open and a middle-aged African American woman appeared.

"Hello?" she said to Chanel.

Two kids ran noisily up the stairs behind her, and the woman called, "I told y'all to stop running in the house!" Then she turned back to Chanel and smiled.

"Hello," Chanel said hesitantly. "I'm

looking for Dorinda Thomas, but I must have the wrong . . ."

"No, she's here. Dorinda!"

A moment later, Dorinda appeared. A little girl with huge brown eyes trotted after her. Dorinda looked surprised—and not exactly pleased—to see Chanel standing on her doorstep.

"Hey, Chanel," she said. Then she turned to the older woman. "Mom, this is my friend, Chanel. Remember I told you about the Cheetah Girls?"

"Oh, yes," the woman said, smiling hugely. "Hi, honey!"

Just then, the sound of breaking glass rang through the apartment, and a chorus of kids cried, "Ooooh . . ."

The woman sighed. "I told you not to touch that!" she called over her shoulder. "Nice to meet you, honey," she said to Chanel before hurrying off.

"Dorinda," said Twinkle, "let's go see somebody get in trouble!"

"You go," Dorinda said, "and I'll be there in

a second, okay?" Twinkle trotted off, and Dorinda stepped into the alley beside Chanel. "If I'd known you were coming, I'd have, um," she shook her head, "been really, really rich and lived somewhere else."

Chanel frowned in confusion. "What?"

Dorinda gestured to her front door. "Now you know why I never invite you guys over or talk about my family."

"I'm really surprised at you, Dorinda," Chanel said as she leaned her bags against a chain-link fence. "Why did you try to hide it?"

"You guys are all, well . . ." Dorinda closed her eyes and sighed. "I guess I didn't think about it."

Chanel giggled. "Wait until I tell Galleria. I mean, the way you dance, you had to have some flavor somewhere." Dorinda shook her head, but Chanel kept talking. "But she said, 'no'—"

"We're not talking about the same thing," Dorinda said, cutting her off.

"So you're half black," Chanel said. "You've

seen Galleria's mom and dad. And I'm a little bit of every kind of Spanish pepper. Shoot, Miss America has ten different bloodlines."

"No!" Dorinda rolled her eyes. "No . . ."

"We're all mixed up together in this jiggy jungle," Chanel went on, "so join the club, girlina-rina."

"Can you just wait for a second?" Dorinda demanded. "I'm not black, or half black, I'm not even white—I don't even know *what* I am. I do know Mrs. Bosco isn't my mom." There was a catch in her voice, and she had to struggle to go on. "But she's the closest I've ever had. My real mom didn't want me." Tears pooled in Dorinda's eyes. "I'm a foster child. I live here with ten other kids. We can only live here because Mr. Bosco is the super. But I want to stay here in this house, and at our school, and with the Cheetah Girls for a while . . ." Dorinda swallowed hard. "Because it's the best I've ever had, Chanel. So please . . . don't take it from me."

"Oh, snaps," Chanel said gently. "You thought we would pull your card for lack of

parents?" Her chest felt tight as she thought about her own mother. "Girl, sometimes that sounds like a good thing."

"Trust me," Dorinda replied. "It's not all it's cracked up to be. You should be grateful that you have a mom."

Chanel tucked a loose strand of Dorinda's hair behind her ear. "Do, you're a Cheetah Girl because of who you are, and what's in your heart. And you are pure Cheetah, *pura vida!*" She wrapped her friend in a warm hug, and felt Dorinda's weight as she sagged against her.

"Look at us," Chanel said as she wiped a tear from her face.

Dorinda giggled through her tears. "You didn't come here to hear my secrets, did you?"

"Nah," Chanel said. "I felt really bad about what happened with Galleria. She gets testy and touchy when she wants everything to be perfect. I wanted to make sure you were okay."

Just then, Twinkle poked her head out

the door and shouted, "Do! Come and eat!"

"I'll be there in a second," Dorinda called, and Twinkle disappeared inside the house. "I'm all right," Dorinda told Chanel. "But I can't look the way she wants me to. I don't have money to buy a new outfit."

Chanel smiled. "Or you can wear this." She handed Dorinda a bag. "I saw it in the window and I thought one of us had to have it."

"Wow," Dorinda whispered as she pulled out a cheetah-print vest.

"Growl power!" Chanel said, laughing. "Let's just say it's on loan from the Juanita and Chanel collection."

"Thanks, girl," Dorinda said, hugging Chanel. "Look," she said as she pulled away, "there's something I need to tell you."

"Tell me what?" Chanel asked, worried. "Are you okay?"

"Yeah," Dorinda said, smiling. "I'm great, actually. I got an offer from the Gold Medal Crew. They want me to dance with them on their summer tour. They want to hire me, Chanel!"

"Oh my gosh! That's great!" Chanel exclaimed.

"I know," Dorinda agreed, "but . . ."

"But . . ." Chanel's smile disappeared as she realized what Dorinda was saying. "What about the Cheetah Girls?"

Dorinda sighed. "Chanel, I really need that money. I just . . . I really don't know what to do."

Chanel swallowed hard. Why did it seem like just as everything was coming together, everything had started falling apart?

11

✿ ✿ ✿ ✿ ✿ ✿ ✿ ✿ ✿ ✿ ✿ ✿ ✿ ✿ ✿ ✿

"Not too much arch," Chanel insisted as Galleria plucked her eyebrows. It was the night before their first official demo rehearsal, and they were primping like mad. Chanel was just worried that Galleria would get carried away . . . which she seemed to be doing a lot these days. "I don't want to look like," she gasped and lifted her eyebrows superhigh, "the Mary J. Blige tickets are all sold out?"

"There." Galleria tweezed out the last renegade hair and sat back to survey her work. "From furry to fierce. They're cheetah-licious. Aren't they, Toto?"

Toto barked in agreement.

"Galleria's day spa," Dorothea said as she walked into Galleria's room, "you girls don't sit up all night gabbing."

"Okay," Chanel said.

"And I've made a decision that . . ." Dorothea looked at the ceiling as though the decision was one she was sure that she would regret. ". . . you can go to the rehearsal alone."

Gasping, Galleria flung her arms around her mother's neck. "Oh, thank you so much!"

"I just want to see how you handle yourselves," Dorothea said. "I'm trusting you."

Chanel hugged her godmother. "Thank you. 'Night, Madrina."

"You're welcome," Dorothea said, then turned to the poofy white dog and added sternly, "Toto, get to bed and be an example to these girls."

Toto scurried to his cheetah-print bed and lay down.

"All right, get some sleep," Dorothea said as she retreated. "Love you."

"Love ya," Galleria called after her. "Oh!" Once her mother was gone, Galleria hurried over to her desk and pulled out a CD. "I wanted to show you this," she said, handing the disk to Chanel. "I want to know what you think."

Chanel studied the cover. "Don't you think there's something wrong with the picture?" she asked slowly.

Galleria leaned in for a better look. "What?"

Chanel frowned. The front of the CD featured a stylish photo of the Cheetah Girls— but one Cheetah in particular was way out in front. "Like, why is there one person in the middle, and why is that person you?"

"Okay," Galleria admitted, "my picture is bigger than everybody else's. But hey . . . I did write the songs." She took the CD and put it on her side table.

"Some of the lyrics were my ideas, too," Chanel shot back. "And Aqua freestyled a lot of the hooks you used. Those were *our* songs."

"Look, I take bits and pieces from outer space and put it all together," Galleria countered as she and Chanel turned down the bed. "I'm an artist."

"And while you're being the artist and taking all the bows, what am I?" Chanel demanded. "Your sidekick? Your flunky?"

"Hey, calm down, Chanel," Galleria said. "Can't we stay focused on the dream?"

Chanel stood there in her cheetah-print pajamas, unable to believe what she was hearing. "Stop trying to handle me. I wasn't born to wipe your shoes and go along with your okey-doke, okay? I'm not the only one feeling it. Aqua and Do are feeling it, too."

"The Cheetah Girls are opening the box behind my back?" Now it was Galleria's turn to be mad.

"You don't hear it when it's in your face, girl." Chanel sat down on the bed next to her best friend. "Look, Bubbles," she said gently, "you're not very much fun right now."

Galleria sighed. "I know, girl," she said patting Chanel's shoulder. "But I promise, everybody will be so happy when we sign that deal tomorrow."

Chanel shook her head, but she dropped it for the time being. "Bubbles," she said slowly, "I found out why Do keeps her life on the DL. She's a foster child. Her mom gave her away when she was a baby."

"What?" Galleria whispered.

"This is no dream, all right? This is the real deal for her."

"Well, then I guess she needs this dream more than anybody, huh?" Galleria said, half to herself.

"No, Bubbles, what she needs are *friends*," Chanel said. "We all do."

"Chuchie." Galleria looked at her best friend from beneath her long lashes. "Friends help friends make their dream come true, right?"

Chanel shrugged. "I guess."

"Well, don't worry about it, girl," Galleria said. "And I'm sure Jackal will have some ideas about the cover tomorrow." She gave Chanel a hug, then turned out the light.

Chanel leaned back against the pile of pillows and stared up at the darkened ceiling. She just couldn't help feeling that she and Galleria weren't talking about the same thing at all.

12

"Cheetah Girls!" Jackal said brightly the next morning as he paced the stylish conference room at Def Duck Records. "I've got a few ideas. And so does my marketing team. Give a listen."

A woman with a sleek, cropped haircut stepped forward. "Our research says your demographic responds to the animal theme. *And* your up-tempo, bouncy, pop-urban sensibility."

Galleria smiled as she folded her arms across her chest. These marketing types know what they're about, she thought smugly. They know the Cheetahs got flair.

The dreadlocked guy spoke up next. "Kids love endangered species. Kids want to party. Kids want a band like . . ."

"Global Getdown!" the marketing team chirped together.

The Cheetah Girls exchanged looks. Global Getdown? Galleria thought. What is this wackitude?

"The letter G is big this year," Dreadlocks explained as Choppy Haircut whipped open a briefcase. He reached in and pulled out a spotted feline mask.

"Galleria stays a cheetah, now and forever," he said, handing the mask to Galleria, who frowned. "Dorinda is a sweet panda," Dreadlocks continued, pulling out more masks. "Here's a baby seal for Aqua, of course. And Chanel is a snow leopard from the frigid north. Brr!"

"Masks?" Chanel asked, taking her snow leopard face hesitantly.

"Our engineering team wants to create whole new identities," Choppy Haircut explained.

"You want us to be something other than the Cheetah Girls?" Chanel asked doubtfully.

"Global Getdown is a worldwide marketing miracle!" Jackal said enthusiastically. "I'm seeing dolls, movie tie-ins with every kind of burger, taco, and anything you can eat with chopsticks." He grinned.

"Well," Dorinda said hesitantly, holding up the panda mask, "how does it look?"

Aqua shook her head.

"Aww, precious," Choppy Haircut said.

"Dorinda, take that off," Galleria commanded. "Jackal, we couldn't even sing in these things."

"You'd be miked inside," Jackal explained. "The music will be on tape, anyway."

"Oh, I'm sorry," Galleria said, "we don't lip-synch."

"Don't worry!" Jackal put his arms around his marketing lackeys. "We'll teach you. Now let's talk music."

"Now we're talking," Galleria said, dropping the mask on the table. Finally—something she knew that she and Jackal were on the same page about. "Cheetahs—'Girl Power!'" She handed a CD to one of Jackal's bodyguards. "Bump this."

The music started to play, and the Cheetahs hit their opening poses. Galleria smiled as she and the other Cheetahs sang and worked Dorinda's dance moves. This number was tight—all of the girls had it on auto-dial. How could Jackal not love it? Galleria thought as she belted out the words. Besides, this song is Toto-approved.

"Excellent," Jackal said when they finished. "Excellent. I loved it. That's exactly the flavor we're looking for."

The Cheetahs grinned at each other. They had nailed it!

"Now," Jackal went on, "here's the song we're looking at. Check this out." A screen descended from the ceiling, and a picture of a girl in a cheetah mask appeared before them. As chirpy music rang through the conference room, Jackal said, "Def Duck Records presents Global Getdown: 'All Around the World'! This is going to go platinum, titanium, uranium. It is animal-friendly, vegetable-friendly, mineral-friendly—this is brilliant! I can smell the millions."

A girl with a seal mask appeared on screen and the chirpy music kept playing. "*All around the world! We go all around the world!*" Jackal sang as he and his marketing team danced around. "*All around the world!* Come on, sing it!"

The Cheetahs stared at the screen, dumb-founded.

Dorinda looked skeptically at Aqua, but after a moment they started singing along with the song. It wasn't easy—it was the lamest beat ever. But they were trying to make the best of it.

Chanel joined in, singing along with Dorinda and Aqua. After all, this was their big chance. And Jackal knows what he's doing, Chanel reasoned. We should listen to him. The song isn't so bad, really, she thought. In fact, it kind of gets stuck in your head after a while, and . . .

"No!" Galleria shouted suddenly. "No! No! No!"

Everyone stopped singing and stared at her.

"Jackal, didn't you like what we just sang?" Galleria asked.

"I loved it," Jackal said. "It was great. But that's not what we sold the record company."

"Well, I'm sorry," Galleria said firmly. "We can't change the Cheetah Girls."

Jackal pulled off his blue shades and gestured to the screen behind him. "This is what they're interested in. This is what they're paying for."

"Well, fine," Galleria said. "Then we bounce." She turned on her heel and strode toward the door.

It took her a moment to realize that the other Cheetahs weren't behind her. She turned to face them, a look of confusion and anger on her face.

"Uh, could you excuse us for a second, please?" Chanel asked Jackal.

"Sure," Jackal said brightly as he and his marketing team headed out. "Guys, let's give these girls a chance to think about that world tour. . . ."

"Why didn't you guys back me up?" Galleria demanded once the door had closed behind them.

"You mean rubber stamp you?" Dorinda snapped. "You're not even giving us time to think."

Galleria rolled her eyes. "Think about what? These are puppets, Do. Besides, now we're one hundred percent down for the talent show. If we win, we still have our demo!"

Aqua folded her arms across her chest. "Don't front, Bubbles. Now you're all gung ho for the talent show?"

"Maybe we have to do things his way at first to get our shot," Chanel put in. "He knows the business. I really think we should consider it."

"It's a job singing and dancing and making people happy," Dorinda added. "What's wrong with that?"

Galleria shook her head. "It's not our music."

"It's not *your song* so you want to walk," Aqua corrected. She turned to Chanel. "You didn't handle this. Now I will." Elbowing Chanel aside, Aqua stepped right up to Galleria. "You're just mad because he won't do your material, right?"

"*Our* material," Galleria said. "Not that 'Everywhere, all around the world' nonsense he's playing."

"You might be right, Galleria." Aqua shrugged. "But you can't speak for the whole group. We make our decisions together."

"You're just one person," Dorinda added, "not the boss of everything."

"Somebody has to be the boss!" Galleria cried. "Somebody needs to remind you why we started the Cheetah Girls. To make our dreams come true our way, not his. Why don't you guys believe in what we have?"

"I wish I could believe in you, Galleria, I really do," Chanel shot back. "But you've been all about *you* lately, and when is it going to stop? I can't . . ." She looked at Dorinda and Aqua and corrected herself. "*We* can't trust you anymore."

"Oh," Galleria said softly, feeling a little

stunned. She had thought that she and the other Cheetahs were on the same page . . . but it sure didn't sound that way. "Okay, well." She smiled weakly. "Problem solved. I'm taking myself out of the equation."

"Come on, Galleria." Dorinda's voice was harsh. "Will you squash the drama?"

"No, really," Galleria insisted. "This is your shot. You need this and I definitely do not want to stand in your way. You guys are on your own." She swallowed hard. "You take the deal." Turning slowly, she reached for the door.

The Cheetah Girls watched her go.

"Did we lose a Cheetah?" Jackal asked gently as he stepped back into the room.

" 'Fraid so," Chanel admitted.

"Happens all the time," Jackal said. "Don't worry, there's more where she came from."

Chanel gaped at him. "Huh?"

"Sure. We can always find another singer. And then . . ." Jackal put his hands on Chanel's shoulders. ". . . move our other lead singer to center mike. Chanel and the Global Getdown."

Chanel touched her hair self-consciously. Center mike? she thought. Well—why not? After all, the group would need a new leader. . . .

Just then, Aqua gave Chanel a little slap on the shoulder, snapping her back to reality. "What?" Chanel said to Jackal. "Sorry, this is too much for one day. I really think we should all think about this."

"Okay," Jackal said. "Well, come back when you're ready for prime time."

Sighing, Chanel walked out of the confer-ence room, followed by Aqua and Dorinda. They were silent as they trooped down the hall and into the lobby, where they were sud-denly overwhelmed by the sounds of chatter and laughter. Several girl groups were there—all waiting to talk to Jackal.

I guess Galleria isn't the only one who can be replaced, Chanel thought as she stared at the groups of girls. They were all in the same boat.

13

When Chanel walked into her apartment, she found her mother sitting on the couch, sorting through a pile of credit card receipts. Chanel's new clothes were everywhere. There was no doubt about it—Chanel was busted.

"What's up, Mom?" Chanel asked carefully.

"What's up?" Juanita demanded, slapping down the receipts. "My credit card balance is up. I got declined! I bought some sandals and I wanted to wear them out of the store. The woman snatched them back so fast she took the paint off my toes. Why did you do this, huh? Why?"

"Ma, I'm sorry," Chanel said. "I'll take it all

back. I thought we were going to be rich soon because of the demo. I'll work and pay you back."

Juanita held up her hand. "I trusted you. I trusted you and you took advantage of me."

"I trusted *you*," Chanel shot back. "I trusted you to pay attention, Ma!"

"You did this because I broke a shopping date?" Juanita asked

"No!" Chanel insisted. "Because Luc came into the picture and it seemed like my dreams didn't matter." Chanel's eyes filled with tears. Her heart felt like it was about to split in two. "But I've seen what it's like not to have a mom," she wailed.

"What?" Juanita stood up and touched her daughter's face. "Honey, calm down. Who doesn't have a mom?"

"It doesn't matter," Chanel said through her tears. "But for now, I just want to thank you for always keeping me in your dreams." Juanita wrapped her daughter in a hug as Chanel went on, "No matter where they take us. Paris, Bucnos Aires. . . . It doesn't matter anymore." Chanel's voice broke. She could hardly force out the words. "The Cheetah Girls are over!"

On the other side of town, Galleria could barely hold back tears as she let herself into her house. But as soon as she saw her mother, the dams burst. "Mom," she cried, "please don't say I told you so!" Dorothea stood up and hugged her daughter as Galleria sobbed on her mother's shoulder.

"I wrote the song," Galleria told her parents as soon as she'd calmed down enough to explain what had happened. "I worked on our look. I had everything buttoned down. I thought we were all on the same page."

"You did what you thought was right, and so did they, honey," Francobollo told her.

"It isn't worth ruining your friendship," Dorothea added.

"How can we be friends again?" Galleria demanded. "They want to be famous. But there are ways, and then there are ways. And I want fame the Cheetah Girls way."

"The Cheetah Girls way," Francobollo asked gently, "or your way?"

"We worked too hard to give it all up," Galleria insisted. "I have to stand up for what's right."

Dorothea looked at her sadly. "I tried so hard to protect you from getting your dreams crushed. But I can't protect you from this heartache. Sometimes you have to let go and let the people you love make their own choices, even if you don't agree with them. I had to learn that with you, and now you have to learn it with your friends."

"What difference is it going to make?" Galleria asked with a sigh. "You either dance with the devil or you don't. And I said no. And I was right, Mom. I was right, wasn't I?"

Galleria sat down at the keyboard in the school auditorium and played a few notes. She began to sing the slow, soulful beginning of the song she'd written for the Cheetah Girls. But after a few lines, she stopped. She just couldn't go on.

"No, keep going," said a voice. It was Derek. He had been watching from the audience. "It wasn't . . . entirely . . . all that bad," he said. "Really. That sounds like something. Not that pop fluff you're usually working."

"You liked it?" Galleria asked.

"Yeah." Derek joined her at the keyboard. "You had somebody write you a Cheetah jam?"

"Uh, no," Galleria said, holding out the sheet music. "I wrote it. All by myself. That's the kind of song Jackal Johnson *didn't* want us to record. He had other ideas for us. Like this, listen to this." She played a few bars of the chirpy Global Getdown song. "*We go all around the world! All around the world!*" she sang. Derek grabbed her hand, stopping her, and Galleria sighed. "It was drama and kaflamma. There were masks involved. And when he asked us to lip-synch, I walked."

"So it's true, huh?" Derek asked with a wry smile. "No more Cheetahs in the jungle?"

Galleria had to laugh. "The Cheetahs are extinct," she admitted. "Oh, I shouldn't be laughing."

"Welcome to the world of a true artist," Derek said. "You really do have to walk alone sometimes. But you've got what it takes to walk." Derek put his arm around her, and Galleria smiled.

"Wait a second," Galleria said suddenly, shrugging off his hug. "You're not just saying that because now you might win the talent show?"

"Yes, I am," Derek said with a completely straight face. "Well," he added, smiling softly, "not completely."

Galleria felt a blush spread from her cheeks all the way to her toes.

Maybe Derek isn't such a big jerk, after all, she thought.

14

❧ ❧ ❧ ❧ ❧ ❧ ❧ ❧ ❧ ❧ ❧ ❧ ❧ ❧ ❧ ❧ ❧ ❧

Dorothea drew her arm through her daughter's as they walked Toto down the street on Saturday afternoon. "I thought we'd spend this evening cuddled up, family-style. Your dad will whip up something delicious, and we'll pop in your favorite movie. . . ." She smiled. "There's no place like home."

Toto barked.

"Thanks, Mom," Galleria said, "but not even the *Wizard of Oz* can fix things now." She still couldn't believe the Cheetah Girls were over. She hadn't spoken to her friends in days, and she wasn't sure she'd ever be able to again. "I was thinking that Toto and I could go down to the talent show and show Drinka some support."

"That's wonderful, honey," Dorothea said. "I'm so proud of you."

"Thanks," Galleria said shyly. "I'll see you."

Giving her mom a wave, Galleria and Toto headed down the street. Suddenly, a poster in a CD store caught Galleria's eye—a life-sized display of four figures in animal masks. Jackal Johnson's photo was at the bottom. GLOBAL GETDOWN, the sign read.

"They went ahead without me," Galleria said slowly. "Toto, can you believe it?"

At that moment, Toto darted away, pulling the leash right out of Galleria's hand.

"Toto!" Galleria cried, but her dog didn't come back. He was already halfway down the block. Frantic, she ran after him, shouting, "Toto! Toto!" Galleria didn't even notice when she ran into a police officer, causing him to spill coffee all over himself. "Toto!"

Finally, Galleria caught up to the sound of barking. She was at a construction site—and Toto had fallen down a hole. "Oh, no! Toto!"

Galleria whipped out her cell phone and dialed. "Dad! Listen to me—Toto is in a hole. Oh! There's a police officer!" Galleria shouted as she caught sight of the policeman who she had run into earlier. "Officer! Officer! Come quick! Please help! My dog Toto, he's in a hole!"

"Dog in a hole?" the officer repeated. He strode over and peered down at Toto. "That's bad. I have to call for backup. Uh, unit fifteen. I've got a dog in a hole by Manhattan Magnet."

Minutes later, news crews and fire trucks were swarming the construction site. "Okay, there he is!" shouted a firefighter as someone lowered a camera into the hole. "A little to the left. Got himself wedged in there good!"

"Toto!" Galleria called. "We're coming to get you! He's not barking anymore—why isn't he barking anymore?"

"We've gotten some oxygen to him," the firefighter assured her. "He'll be okay while we figure all this out."

A news reporter stood in front of a nearby

TV camera. "Hal Hartman here in downtown where we're getting to the bottom of the traffic jam that's paralyzing midtown. Apparently, Toto is not in Kansas anymore."

"Galleria!"

Turning, Galleria saw her father shouting in Italian at a firefighter who wouldn't let him through. A crowd had gathered, and the police and firefighters were trying to hold the people back.

"Oh! These are my parents!" Galleria explained. She led them over to the TV monitor that had been set up, so they could watch Toto. He looks scared, Galleria thought, staring at the little dog on the screen.

Suddenly, Aqua appeared. "How are you, Mrs. Garibaldi?" she said to Galleria's mother. "How's Toto?"

Galleria's eyes widened. "How did you know?"

"You're all over the news!" Aqua explained.

Galleria looked around her, where lines of cars were honking like crazy. "But the traffic's all tied up. How did you get down here?"

Aqua's eyes flicked to the nearby subway sign, and Galleria gasped.

"Did you take the train for me?" Galleria asked.

"I took the train for Toto," Aqua said simply. "I'm from Texas. I learned from the Rangers. We never leave a man—or a dog—behind. Hang in there, baby boy!" she called to Toto.

Just then, Dorinda came running up.

"Do!" Galleria cried.

"Hey! Is he all right?" Dorinda asked peering into the hole beside Aqua. "Ooh, doesn't look good."

"Excuse me! Excuse me!" A woman and a girl in curlers were pushing through the edge of the crowd.

"Chuchie!" Galleria shouted, realizing that one of those sets of curlers belonged to Chanel. The other belonged to Juanita. They had busted out of the beauty parlor when they saw Toto on the news. "Thanks for coming!"

"How did this happen?" Chanel demanded. "Did you let him off the leash?"

"Hold up," Aqua said calmly. "We've got one disaster here, we don't need another one."

"Somebody finally sticks up for me!" Galleria threw her arms around Aqua. "Thank you!"

"I mean her hair," Aqua snapped, starting to pull Chanel's curlers out. "Losing track of Toto—I blame you."

"You guys, this isn't my fault!" Galleria insisted.

"Nothing ever is," Chanel shot back.

"His head is drooping!" Dorinda cried as she watched Toto. "Do something!"

"We might have to cut into the street," a firefighter explained. "We turned the neighborhood gas off, and they're cutting the power off now." He gave a signal to the other firefighters.

"Following our story on the crazy gridlock surrounding the Manhattan Magnet School," Hal Hartman went on, narrating the crazy scene. "Totowatch continues. Will they get him out in time?"

"Galleria," said a husky voice next to her.

"Drinka!" Galleria looked around. Suddenly she realized that she was surrounded by people from her school. Everyone was there—including Derek and Mackerel. "Why's everyone here? What happened to the talent show?" she asked.

"It's all right, honey." Drinka lifted her eyebrows. "Somebody shut down the power."

"Oh," Galleria said softly. Now there was yet another thing that was her fault—she had ruined the talent show. "I just wanted to say, I'm sorry," she told Drinka. "Everything's my fault. I'm sorry I got a big head."

"It's okay." Drinka nodded. "Yeah, you got a big head. It's full of dreams . . . and you got a big heart to match it. But—you need to watch out about that big mouth."

Smiling, Galleria reached out and hugged her teacher, who hugged back. "It's going to be all right," Drinka promised.

"We've opened up a little space there," a firefighter called as he peered in at Toto's

limp form, "but he's not moving. You're going to have to get in here and call to him."

Galleria scrambled toward the hole, and the other Cheetahs followed. They all called to Toto at once.

"He can't hear you!" the firefighter shouted.

"Okay, 'Together,'" Dorinda said.

Galleria knew exactly what she meant. She began to sing the opening lines of the Cheetah Girls' song, "Together."

"That's it!" the firefighter called. "He's moving—that's it!"

The other Cheetahs joined in. Then the crowd started clapping along, and the firefighter urged them, "Faster! He's wiggling, he's wiggling! Sing faster! I've almost got him!"

Cheetah voices rose into the air as the girls sang their hearts out.

"I got him!" The firefighter held up a very dirty, smudgy Toto, and the crowd erupted into cheers.

"Oh, thank you!" Galleria cried as she hugged Toto to her chest. "Thank you!"

"Baby!" Dorinda said, petting Toto's ears. "We're so glad you're okay."

Chanel looked up at Galleria. "I'm glad he's okay," she said quietly. A moment later, she and the other two Cheetahs turned and started slowly into the crowd. Galleria stared after them sadly.

"Hey!" Derek broke through the crowd, and hurried up to Galleria. "They all came running when you sent out the Cheetah distress signal."

"No," Galleria said. "They came running for Toto. The Cheetah Girls, they're actually over. You know what? You're right. I have to walk alone."

Derek took Galleria's hands in his. "You know you were right to walk away from Jackal's offer."

"I know I was." Galleria sighed. "I was right."

"But now there's only one question," Derek went on. "Are you right to walk away from your friends?"

Galleria stared up into Derek's eyes. When

did he get to be so smart? she wondered. Suddenly, she had an idea. Leaning over, she whispered in his ear. He nodded and hurried into the Manhattan Magnet auditorium.

Galleria decided she wanted to sing one last song for the Cheetahs . . . for her friends. She opened her mouth and began to sing the soulful beginning of the new song.

Hearing her, Dorinda stopped in her tracks. She turned back and began to sing. Then Aqua added her voice.

Galleria looked up in surprise. They were listening. They were hearing her.

Aqua reached for Galleria's hands. Aqua, Dorinda, and Galleria embraced as they kept singing.

Chanel found herself walking through the crowd toward her friends, and the words burst from her before she even realized she was singing. At once, the girls were in perfect harmony.

The crowd applauded. Just then, a wailing guitar rift cut through the night air, picking up the beat. It was Derek—he'd gone back into the auditorium to get his electric guitar. Now he played for the Cheetah Girls, and the Cheetahs burst into their choreographed performance.

Toto went crazy, dancing on his hind legs, and the crowd cheered wildly, clapping and shouting as the Cheetah Girls worked the song, right up until the last note.

Galleria smiled at her friends. They were back together! Okay, maybe it was just for one song—but even if the Cheetah Girls were gone, at least she had her friends back. Galleria looked gratefully at Derek, and he leaned over and kissed her.

Seeing them, the other Cheetahs let out a whoop. It was the happy ending they had all been waiting for.

15

"So," Galleria said uncertainly later in the Manhattan Magnet auditorium. Once the power came back on, everyone had returned to the school for juice and cookies. "We're still friends, even if the Cheetah Girls are over?"

"The Cheetah Girls are over?" chorused the other girls.

"Girl, I can't take no more news flashes!" Aqua said. "Come on, now!"

"But I saw the Global Getdown sign," Galleria told her. "You guys took the deal. I can't say that I blame you."

"Girl, we didn't take that deal!" Aqua cried.

"We let some other puppet heads take that. Believe that."

"But, Do, are you all right with money?" Chanel asked. "I mean, what about the Gold Medal Crew?"

Dorinda grinned. "I'm taking over the beginner dance classes while my instructor goes on tour. I'm waiting for the real Cheetah cheddar. With my girls."

"We're still Cheetah!" Chanel cried. "*Pura vida*, mama!"

"*Pura vida!*" the Cheetahs chimed, clinking their plastic cups of juice.

"Dorinda!" Twinkle and Mrs. Bosco hurried over to the Cheetah Girls. "Can I be a Cheetah Girl this time, too?" Twinkle asked.

Dorinda smiled. "This is Mrs. Bosco," she told the Cheetahs, "my foster mother. And this is my family."

Hearing her, Dorothea embraced Mrs. Bosco. "Oh, welcome! We need more Cheetah-mamas in this jiggy jungle!"

"Whoo-hoo!" Drinka called suddenly, taking the stage. "Announcement! Announcement!

By overwhelming and unanimous decision, the Manhattan Magnet Talent Show First Prize goes to . . . the Cheetah Girls!"

The Cheetahs cheered and the crowd applauded as the girls accepted their disco-ball trophy.

We got the demo! Galleria realized. We did it! And we didn't have to sell out.

Just then, Galleria's cell phone rang. "Yes?" she said, tossing her long hair over her shoulder. "Cheetah-world, Galleria speaking!" Galleria's eyes went wide. "Jackal Johnson calling?" She hesitated a minute, unsure what to say. She wanted to tell him to get lost, but she didn't want to speak for the group. . . .

Chanel grabbed the phone. "Hello? Tell him the Cheetah Girls don't run with wolves or hang with hyenas."

Aqua took the phone and added her own piece of wisdom. "You tell him the Cheetah Girls don't follow anybody's dreams but their own, and nobody else's, honey."

"You know what?" Galleria added, taking the phone back. "Tell him the Cheetah Girls depend on family and friends and the growl power of all the cheetah-licious divas who came before us to see us through."

Now it was Dorinda's turn. "Tell him the Cheetah Girls are gonna be stars our way, our day."

"Just tell him the Cheetah Girls are un-available," Galleria finished, hanging up.

The Cheetahs burst into cheers, and Galleria grinned. She was back with her Cheetah sisters. And that was never going to change.

Groove to the sound of all your favorite shows

Disney Channel Soundtrack Series

Disney's
Kim Possible
TV Soundtrack

The Cheetah Girls
TV Soundtrack

Lizzie McGuire
TV Soundtrack

Pixel Perfect
Soundtrack

Also, look for...

- ### *The Proud Family* TV Series Soundtrack
- ### *That's So Raven* TV Series Soundtrack

Collect them all!

www.DisneyRecords.com
Available Wherever Music Is Sold.

Wake up.
Go to school.
Save the world.

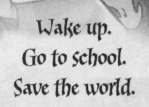

W.í.t.c.h

Will   Irma   Taranee   Cornelia   Hay Lin

The magic of friendship

The new book series · Make some powerful friends at *www.clubwitch.com*